TIME TOGETHER

Me and Mum

BY MARIA CATHERINE

ILLUSTRATED BY PASCAL CAMPION

THIS BOOK BELONGS TO:

Libary Queens Park

Cosy story time

Tasty cooking time

Carefree summer time

Splish splash
bubble time

What-to-wear time

Food adventure time

Creative quiet time

Fly high time

Squeeze tight time

Beauty salon time

Chugga-chugga choo-choo time

Secret sharing time

Sweet dream time

Raintree is an imprint of Capstone Global Library Limited, a
company incorporated in England and Wales having its registered
office at 7 Pilgrim Street, London, EC4V 6LB – Registered
company number: 6695582

www.raintreepublishers.co.uk
myorders@raintreepublishers.co.uk

ISBN 978 1 406 27571 1
Printed in China by Nordica.
1013/CA21301928
17 16 15 14 13
10 9 8 7 6 5 4 3 2 1

British Library Cataloguing in Publication Data
A full catalogue record for this book is available from the British
Library.

Concept by: Kay Fraser and Christianne Jones
Designer: K. Fraser

Photo credits: Shutterstock